# Bar Yarns for the Average American
Nikki Boss

abuddhapress@yahoo.com

ISBN: 9798713790677

# Table of Contents

# Physics of Marriage

"On the dresser." She spoke slowly.

"I've already looked there."

She sipped at her cigarette, afraid to pull too deep. "Well, look again."

"Where are my keys? I'm going, Tessa."

"So go." She raised her chin, blowing smoke toward the center of the room.

*

Buoyancy causes cigarette smoke to spread through the air in layers; non-zero velocity also plays a part. When a smoker exhales, the smoke rises because the temperature is higher than that of the air, but cools as it does so, decreasing the net force. The smoke appears stagnant, though it is still moving. It is the air that is stagnant.

*

"Enjoy your whore, Sam." She ground her cigarette into the clamshell ashtray, one singular movement of strength. Tessa could keep creating ashes, and she could blow them all away with a single breath.

"I need my keys, Tessa."

"I need my husband." She wrapped her arms around herself and held on tight. "It's been over twenty years. I'm your *wife*."

"Fine. I'll call a cab, then."

She screamed. The neighbors downstairs slammed a door. Outside, a taxi honked. The city traffic was melodious in an orchestra of noise.

\*

Pitch, frequency, intensity, speed -- words associated with sound. Variations in pressure cause sound waves to travel – an object vibrates, causing the air to vibrate, causing the eardrum to vibrate. The brain connects these vibrations as sound.

\*

Sam lunged at her.

His hands were carrion, they consumed everything in their path. They had consumed Tessa long ago, annihilating any strength she once had.

\*

The tangible fist stops when it connects to the face, but the energy keeps going. The movement must go somewhere. Momentum transfer. Figuring this out mathematically can cradle that energy, using the laws of physics to absorb a punch. Physical equations to decrease physical trauma.

\*

"Just give me the keys. I'll be back at some point." He looked down at her with distaste. She went into the kitchen and opened a cabinet, handing him the keys along with her white flag. He left without another word.

Tessa began twisting the wedding ring on her finger. Back and forth, up and down. The scab underneath reopened.

*

There is an old adage that to see is to believe. Human blood is not blue. Light does not travel through skin without effort. It is absorbed and spit back out continuously. The human eye processes the reflecting light and provides an answer: blue. Light is able to trick the eye, coercing the brain into seeing something that doesn't exist.

*

Sam came back Thursday morning, long after a greenish-blue flower had bloomed against Tessa's cheekbone. He kissed her softly and handed her a rose.

She smiled and lit another cigarette.

# It's Just a Walk in the Park

I love to be in love and I am grateful for it. The park is where things can happen and when I saw her there for the first time, I let my mind unfold. It was sunny out but not hot yet. Hopeful. The snow had melted a few days before. She had this blue scarf on, one of those scarves the girls wear that they loop twice about their necks.

The first time I saw her, in that scarf, she was with a little boy and a man. I was close enough to watch her, close enough to hear her name as she smiled at the man next to her and sat the little boy on a swing. His mittens matched his coat and they kissed and then she pushed him. He went higher and higher and I thought to myself, *she's the one*.

Leah was a mother.

The second time I saw her, she was coming out of this little bodega on the corner of Broadway and 22nd and I thought *there's that girl again* so I smiled. I knew it then, knew it had to be love, because the city is so big and she was so close; it was so obviously a sign. I said hello.

She said hello back and I knew it was love.

Leah was kind.

There is a park I visit to smoke or meet with one of the Internet girls. I look at the stars and I look at the world and I look for love when I am there. I sat there on my bench one night when I didn't have any plans.

But love intervened. I saw Leah under the streetlights; I recognized her right away, her face illuminated under the glow of a street lamp. She was walking alone and I thought to myself, *well that isn't safe*.

Leah was independent.

I called out to her. "Everything okay?"

"What?" she slowed a bit. "Who is that?" Still, she walked towards me.

"It's only me. You okay?" I said it tenderly, letting her know I loved her. "Not a great part of town."

"Yeah…okay, buddy."

Leah was cocky.

"I just want you safe." She was in front of me now, pausing, and I gazed up at her.

"Mess off." She slurred those words, her mouth working oddly against the foul language.

Leah was glorious.

I laughed. "What's your name?"

She kept walking. She was becoming ungrateful.

I told her my name.

"It's late." I added.

"Yes," she said. "Well, see ya."

"Where are you headed?"

She didn't answer. I got off the bench and caught up with her. Her body was aware and picking something up. Vibes.

Leah had good vibes.

I told her then, said her name and then smiled, because I like this part. It's like reading a book but better.

"But I don't know your son's name."

Genuine alarm came into her eyes but her face did not flinch. I admired that.

I admired Leah.

"My friends are just up ahead. " A nervous sound, low and not quite a laugh, came from her throat. I glanced around and saw no one.

Leah was lying.

She started walking faster.

I started walking faster.

"Leah," I sighed. "Don't make this hard."

Leah started to run.

Leah was smart to run.

I chased her.

She ran faster.

I'm stronger.

I got her.

She screamed and it ripped my ears up. Annoying. I punched her in the back of the head; it's the easiest spot. She fell. I did remember my manners and turned her over. I gazed into her eyes and pinned her down

to keep her safe.

"Leah." I was so happy. I wanted to show her my prize, so I did.

Bleeding from the mouth, she whispered, "Please."

"Please what, Leah?" I held it out.

"Please don't do this. Please." she was scared. Ungrateful.

Irresponsible.

"Do what?" I whispered. "I love you, Leah. Tell me you love

me, too."

Tears rolled across her temples from the side of her eyes. It was

infuriating.

I didn't have a choice.

Lights out.

For all her bravado, I had to put her to sleep.

Leah was mine, for a moment.

I left my Leah alone in the park to chance, or fate, or maybe even

God.

That's the last time I'll go for a girl around town. There's

nothing romantic about it. It's nothing like the movies. I'll stick with the

Internet girls. They know the rules.

And then there was this: heading back towards Broadway, I saw

a group of females waiting by the east entrance. Maybe those were

Leah's friends. Leah could have introduced me to them, I thought. We could have had fun together, all of us. They didn't even bother to say hi as I passed.

They could have showed up on time and none of this would have happened.

They weren't her friends.

Ungrateful.

Irresponsible.

Those girls were nothing like my poor Leah, left all alone in the park.

# Flight

The inn is crowded and it takes too long to get outside, where tears can be erased with my palms before they matter. Men pinch and grab as I walk through the room. Each step I take is a syllable, the lament and moan of customer's names. Prostitution: the patron saint in my homeless existence.

I make it to a field behind the inn, alone with the full moon offering solace until footsteps hit my ears. I am afraid and alone in the night.

"Mary." His voice creates pause. My name has become unfamiliar to me; they call me Magdalene. They also call me whore.

I do not know this man before me. Some of the villagers call him Messiah in mockery, but not all. I cannot answer because my voice will suffocate beneath the weight of each man I have lain with.

He offers his hand, and I wonder.

"Walk with me, Mary. Follow." His voice is a request, gentle. I give him my hand, and we walk together without looking back. My sins are named. We stop and watch each one grow wings, and we clap as they take flight.

# Mouse, Party of One

Every day I get to work and there are dead guys all over the floor. I hate those fuckers, with their naked pink tails and stupid broken necks. Most days I don't even want to come in. Dead guys, everywhere.

The kitchen I work at is in a busy corner of the city. It's a dirty little place but I don't mind any, mostly because I'm a dirty boy myself. A dirty bird.

"Roland!" It's the new waitress calling me. The little one; she's cute. "Roland, you got my order up?" She stands with her hip out, glaring at me. I wonder what she would do if I lobbed one of them dead guys at her. Or handed her one on a plate to serve her stupid customers.

"Coming." I try not to say anything I think. Just take it all in. I think and I cook, and I am the dead-mouse boy.  Gross.

A new ticket comes up and I get this funny little idea going, rolling around in my brain. I giggle but not too loud. I got this perfect idea: what fun it would be to take one of them dead boys and serve him up instead.

The order is for a cheeseburger to go and I picture the littlest dead guy of the morning. I can off his tail, easy-peasy-mousey-squeezy, and roll him up inside a burger no problem.

"What's that new waitresses' name?" I ask Peter the prep cook. Peter Piper, Petey Popsicles. Petey the prep cook. He doesn't have to pick up dead mice every morning.

"Angela." Petey the prep cook doesn't even glance up at me as he says it. He just continues chop-chop-chopping away.

"Angela!" I turn and call her name out the kitchen window. She's standing by the counter, perfect ass aimed right in my direction. *Petey Peeper* I think to myself, and another name for Pete the prep cook is born. "Angela, is this order waiting or a pick-up?"

"Yeah." She flicks her eyes up at me. "He's waiting."

I know I gotta act quickly, so I move real quick-like towards the trash and make myself trip over it. Trash spills out but it's only about eleven o'clock so the mess isn't too bad. Just what I needed.

"Chill out, dude." Petey Peepers finally looks up from his prep cooking. "Clean that shit up, customers are looking. You high again, Roland?" I don't say anything back to him, not out loud anyway. Grabbing the broom and brushing the trash back into the bin, I am able to grab that little dead guy and hide him in my apron. It's easy enough to lob his tail off and stuff him up tight into a meat patty.

"Coming right up, Angela." She looks at me and for a sec my ears feel kind of hot. Just real quick, up-at–the-tip-like. I play it smooth though, use my spatula to press the patty down, but not too hard cause I don't want that dead guy's guts leaking out.

"Just a few more minutes." I sing it out to myself.

"Roland! What the fuck, bro." Petey Pink-eyes whispers it. "Roland, you high, dude, or what?"

I just ignore him.

When that burger is ready I slide it onto the bun and grab one of the Styrofoam to-go containers. I'm slicing up the romaine nice and neat, then move on to slices of big red tomato. That produce guy is on point today. Vegetables all fresh looking and shit.

"Order up." I set the container in the server window. "Here's your burger to go."

"Eight ninety-five," Angela tells the customer, this old dude with some weird green hat on. "Out of twenty?" I snicker again and watch this dude leave with his lunch all wrapped up in a paper bag.

"Roland! Chill out, dude!" Petey Popsicles over there is at it again and he's pissing me off some. Just cause a guy might like a bit of a Crystal pick-me-up, Petey here thinks there's something wrong. There *is* something wrong with me, Petey-fucking-petals. All these dead guys are driving me crazy.

I figure I better get going. "Yo, listen up!" I yell it nice and loud. Petey starts hissing at me to shut up. "I'm leaving."

"You're what?" Petey Pipers is at it again.

"I quit. Gotta go. Things to do." I smile real big, showing what a nice guy I am.

He's yammering at me but I just walk through the dining room and grab a soda on my way out. The orange kind, cause it tastes nice. And then I grab Angie's ass as I go, cause I can.

Those fucking dead guys, man. They'll drive you out of a kitchen every time.

# The Other

"When you come back, I will be here like this."

"What does that mean?"

"Nothing to you but everything to me."

"Sarah." I love how he says my name, Say-ruh.

"Come here." I pull him to me, my hands cupping the back of his neck.

He pulls away.

"I have to go."

"You could stay if you wanted to."

"I can do anything I want."

"Except stay with me." And there it is. It does not matter what I want or

what he wants; there will always be this.

He stands and his eyes scan the room.

"In the bathroom," I tell him. He stands to get his clothes and it is in this

moment I light a cigarette. Inhale deeply and let the smoke unfurl from

my mouth.

"Say-ruh."

I ignore him.

"Say-ruh." I will not go to him.

"James." I state his name rather than reply. Take another drag and let it

poison me.

"You can lie in that bed all day and it does nothing."

I spit back. "I can do whatever I want."

The door slams. He is leaving me again.

# Summer is for Lovers

Sweat loitered between her breasts. Pop music played softly from a radio in the corner. Using the back of a wrist, she brushed the hair from her face and asked –

"Just the two chocolate? Anything else?"

" Just those." His eyes flickered up. "You're Josh Sampson's kid." She remembered why the couple looked familiar. The man leaned in towards her. "The boss's daughter." Slowly, a smile broke his face apart. The wife, overweight with messy hair, kept her eyes on the floor.

Candace let her tongue run along her lips, looked him in the eyes. Her shirt clung to her like candy in the heat. The curve of her ice cream scoop rolled the chocolate into a perfect ball. She handed him the first cone and let her fingers linger on his. She meant to hand the second cone to the wife but he grabbed that one too, pretended to drop it. She giggled. He tipped her a five, too much.

"See you around." The wife never looked up, not even as the bells jingled on their way out of the shop. A seagull squawked outside and Candace paused for a minute, watching them walk to their car.

*Why is your wife so fat*, she wanted to ask him when he showed up again three days later. He slipped her his card. *Sampson's Marina*, it read. *John Marles, Dock 4.*

She met him late one night a week after that, after she closed the ice cream shop. He brought her to an abandoned building downtown. Huge metal letters were bracketed to the bricks lining the rumbled old building, K-W-R-X.

"What is this place?" she asked. A glass wall behind them showcased hulking equipment no longer in use. The carpet, rough under her naked body, smelled like urine. He had kissed her, taken her clothes off slowly, and screwed her there on the rug. They lay together now, but Candace wanted more. She always wanted more.

"It's mine. I had a life before the marina." He shifted his body to gaze down at her. "I ran this station, bought this building."

She didn't really care. "What happened?"

"Ran out of money."

"And now you're a dock hand?" Candace grabbed his flaccid penis, put it in her mouth. He swatted her away, agitated. *(Agitated? Who doesn't want their dick sucked?)*

"Only job around."

"Why do you still have this building?" She was getting bored.

"I used everything I had to buy it outright. Been trying to sell it."

"It smells like urine." She reached again for his penis; gave up. Rolling her eyes, she got up and started to dress. "It smells like piss!"

"This station was my home."

"Your home is with a whale." Obviously he didn't want more sex. John Marles was pathetic.

He glared. "Say that again?"

"Your wife is a whale."

"Why are you doing this?" He stood up. She stared at him.

"Doing what?" She slipped her feet into flip-flops and examined her hands. There was a callus on her index finger from the ice cream scoop.

"You're an asshole."

"So are you."

He spit on her.

"What the fuck?" Candace wiped his saliva off her shoulder, smearing it in more than rubbing it off.

"You little slut." He shoved her and she fell on the floor, stunned. For a moment they locked eyes.

She screamed. "You're pathetic!"

He shoved his legs into his jeans, kicked at her and stumbled a bit. She wasn't laughing anymore. "Spoiled little bitch."

"Chubby chaser." She hurled each word and wasn't sure how they had got to this point, wasn't sure if she was safe. "Pedophile."

"You're nothing but a tease." He was too close, right in her face. Candace was afraid to move. She froze and for a moment, they were alone on the earth. She blinked.

John Marles, dock 4, moved first. He walked across the room but did not look at her. The heavy metal door slammed behind him at the same time she remembered they hadn't used a condom.

His white socks lay alone in the corner. She considered, briefly, bringing them with her.

# The Creation of Mary

Mary's nose is too long and her fingers are too stubby, but she walks like a dancer. The enthusiasm Mary holds for life is infectious. She becomes beautiful when you watch her. This beauty drowned, briefly, by way of a man named Domenic.

Once upon a time, Mary believed she + Domenic = love. She counted picket fences and children until falling into sleep laced with movie-dreams, colorful for the future. Now she dreams in shades of grey. She cannot remember who she is.

*(Mary lost her virginity in $9^{th}$ grade to a boy named Albert. Albert and Mary were pledged 2gether 4ever. Senior year: along came Domenic with his black curls and bright green eyes. Mary left Albert, telling him she needed to follow her heart. Albert today: a family practitioner saddled with a three-hundred-pound wife and four kids.)*

Something amazing happens. Mary doesn't give in; she decides she wants herself back. She remembers the family she has become estranged from and calls them. She no longer sees Domenic in her reality. She understands now – this type of love is only an illusion.

Mary waits patiently until she is strong enough to tell Domenic, "I'm leaving now." Her father is there to hold her hand but butterflies live in Mary's stomach and their wings are made of lead.

She packs one bag while Domenic sits at the edge of the bed. He cries. Mary wonders when was the last time she read a book, and she smiles. Her father, guard of the doorway, smiles back. Domenic = a subject for observation. He has become an interesting bug or a temper-ridden toddler.

Swinging her bag onto a slender shoulder, Mary leaves. Domenic slams the bedroom door and walks behind them, begging. Mary's father holds her hand tight and leads her out of the house. There is no kiss good-bye.

*(Domenic begins the destruction of a New Girl, a young woman with large eyes and bad skin. New Girl + Domenic = fierce passion but Domenic = unsure. Sometimes Domenic decides he hates New Girl and elevates his control methods to show her. The relationship quickly evolves: New Girl + Domenic = positive pregnancy test. They hug and smile and will pose for family pictures at Kmart.)*

Mary breathes the air in deeply, and she thinks: *this*. She paints at midnight and cooks pretentious meals for one. Reading for hours during the day, Mary sleeps with whomever she deigns worthy for the night. There is life, full of new places and writing witty vignettes for travel magazines.

Andalusia becomes her favorite place. Mary dances and twirls and eats oranges, plump and vivid. The juice trickles down her arms. She wipes sticky wrists on her skirts and throws her head back when she laughs. Mary wears an anklet made of bells and they jingle quietly, singing to her, as she walks.

# Memories on *Marceline*

*'Jim Jones' and 'killer Kool-Aid' were household words back then…I was being raised as a Jehovah's Witness and we were trying to defend [that] and say that we were not a cult. We were trained we were not a cult, because cults follow a man…those people thought Jim Jones was their prophet, their leader. He was [sic] their Jesus, if you will.*
Tammy, 43, former Jehovah's Witness

*"I've been living on hope a long time."*
Jim Jones
-----

The sun created diamonds across the Atlantic Ocean in November of 1978, light skipping across each wave's crest as it rose and fell like a heartbeat.

"Sarah." I turned at my name. Stepping away from the ship's rail, feet unsteady, the diamonds shifted and became omens.

"It's time." I turned away from the ship's rail and followed the 18-year-old Captain Greg down the hatch, into an empty cargo hold. My hands moved automatically down the ladder rungs one after another, steel ice solid in my grip.

*"And I'd just like to thank Dad for giving us life, and also death…"* A small marine radio in the corner allowed us to hear a man's voice, disconnected and faint, harmonizing with the static.

"Listen."

"Is it…?"

"White Night. It's happening."

We listened carefully, sitting together cross-legged around the radio. The walls were spotted with orange flowers, blooming rust like bullet holes against unforgiving metal. Rays of sunshine streamed down into the hatch, our only light in the cargo hold of the *Marceline*.

Inside my chest, I felt like my heart would explode.

-----

*A lot of people are tired around here, but I'm not sure they're ready to lie down, stretch out and fall asleep.*

*All that's, let me – All they're doing is taking a drink, that takes, to go to sleep ... That's what death is, sleep ... I know, but I'm tired of it all.*

*We didn't commit suicide. We committed an act of revolutionary suicide protesting the conditions of an inhumane world...*

Jim Jones, leader of People's Temple

-----

"*Marceline,* can you hear me? Mary to *Marceline*. Do you copy? Over." Captain Greg uttered a sound, half-formed, words lodged somewhere in his throat. He grasped the receiver with both hands.

"Copy. This is Greg. Over.*"*

"*White Night, White Night. Engage immediately; embody the people. Over.*" And with that code, we would die. We had been commanded to enter a new life through death. That code had been created for one thing. Utopia had fallen.

"Engagement in effect. Greg, Sarah, Al. Over." We looked at one another and our eyes said nothing.

"Um." My throat was dry and I looked at my shipmates for an answer. "I guess the Senator's visit didn't go so well?"

Greg's head turned my way slowly, calculating his next move. "Is that supposed to be funny?"

I cleared my throat. "No, sir. No. I just, ah, I guess we need to join the Temple."

"You guess?" his voice was steady.

"I guess I'm just wondering how...if...what if we stay here?"

"Stay here?"

"Maybe we don't have to, you know..." Al spoke for the first time, but his voice faltered and faded and he never quite finished that sentence. Greg's fists shot out before I could react, his hands flying and ripping at a man he once called brother. Al reacted instantly, lunging at Greg and toppling the two of them to the floor.

They were screamed like pigs in a slaughterhouse -- feral cries debating life and death fifty miles from the Guyana coast, but we had already chosen. I remembered in that moment I had a mother somewhere. I had doubts.

It didn't matter.

-----

*I tell you, you should be happy about this. I was just thinking about Jim Jones. He just has suffered and suffered and suffered. He is the only god and he don't even have a chance to enjoy his death here.*
Unidentified People's Temple Member

*"…when the final time came…anyone who didn't want to commit suicide was held down and shot with needles filled with potassium cyanide. Unless you were one of the lucky ones who happened to sneak off into the jungle, you were dead. They went around with stethoscopes, and if you still had a heartbeat, you'd be shot."*
Teri Buford O'Shea, Survivor

-----

*I'm going to tell you…without me, life has no meaning.*

Jim Jones

-----

# City Minute

"I've been waiting for you for days." Nancy slinks like a cat, one foot in front of the other down concrete steps cracked with age. The steel door shuts quietly behind her.

I have been chain-smoking and looking for non-existent stars under a smog-filled sky, drunkenly wondering why things happen just so. "Have you?"

"I have." She does not sit so much as melt onto the top step. "I knew I would find you." We have been here before, her and I. Her arms wrap around the sweater she wears against her body, an oversize grey cloth like a blanket I want to crawl under or a flag saying: yes.

She looks at me all the time. Her gaze is two degrees from suffocation. It would be unnerving did I not find her so attractive.

"Well…" She told me a few weeks ago I fascinated her; she wanted to start an affair but I should be thinking about the idea of it first, what an affair would mean. Next time I saw her outside smoking a cigarette, I kissed her. Or maybe she kissed me first. We were both drunk so it is not entirely clear. We had sex violently, quickly, against the side of the building. She has lived in my head each day since.

"I'm waiting for more." She lights up a smoke. The tobacco kind. Her drink sloshes over the side of her glass when she moves. How can you resist a girl like that? Always drinking and laughing. Smoke dancing

and un-folding from full lips that she bites purposely when she talks to me. Lips painted with some glossy shit, always staring at me while she puts it on. Each move is thought out, I think, lyrical and intoxicating. She will trap me if I let her.

I tell her I'm not sure.

"What?" she slides down a step and straightens her back. Looks up at me. "You don't know?"

"I don't know if I want the consequences."

"Consequences?"

"The stuff that would come after."

"After what? It already happened."

"Your affair, Nancy. What happens at the end of your affair?"

"Well." She takes a sip of her drink, red wine I'm sure, and sets it carefully on the steps beside her. "It's not just my affair." She pauses to blow smoke towards the stars we cannot see.

"Mine, too." I agree, because Nancy is a girl to be agreed with.

"And?"

"Why can't we leave things where they are?" A fourth cigarette finds my lips; I am desperate to inhale. "You're married, Nancy. I'm the single one here. I can't be that guy."

It's too dark to tell if her face reddens. "All right."

"Nancy." I say it too quickly, and I am scared at the way her name slips so easily from my mouth.

"Like you said, I'm married." I hear it then, the sadness in her voice, and for a moment I forget she is the one playing games.

I wonder if her husband knows she is not solely his. "Nancy, come on."

"What are you drinking?" She reaches for my glass and I hand it to her, watching her lips cover the rim and her mouth work as she swallows the whiskey.

"Preston." She stands. "Come here."

"No." I say it because I have to, for all the nights my mother cried into her own arms wishing they were my fathers, falling asleep at the kitchen table. Vodka and Valium and my father's adultery defined her. "I can't."

"Of course you can. Come here." She reaches for me but I move away and a sound rises from her throat. I know it is anger.

"It's not a good idea."

"Come here!" she says it more forceful, plays with my belt as she moves toward me.

It takes everything I have. "No, Nancy. I already said no."

She steps back, and looks at me, those eyes pouring into me.

I have to say it. "I'm sorry."

She responds with a squint that is more like a glare or a slap to the face but the softer kind, a theatre hit, and then Nancy flicks a half-smoked cigarette to the ground as she turns to open the door. Defiantly.

She pauses in the doorway before she goes. "Fuck off, Preston." I watch her flutter up the stairs, that sweater still wrapped around her body. I almost call her back, but remember just in time: I am not my father.

# Angel Puke

Jecklyn James was a fabulous porn star. Though an incorrigible sinner, Jecklyn loved the Lord with all her heart -- this saved her soul (it wasn't being a Mormon, after all), and she flew to Heaven upon death (angels did, indeed, have wings). Unfortunately, Jecklyn's true nature wasn't particularly conducive to life beyond the pearly gates. After a few hundred years, insolence and snark towards her heavenly peers banished Jecklyn to a small, black space from which she could not quite seem to break free. Whether her time in the hole was meant to be eternal, one could only guess. What Jecklyn did know was that every hundred years, an opening appeared at the top of the hole. Each time the hole appeared above, she tried to spread her wings and fly through but it never worked. Was it Hell? Maybe.

Last time the hole opened, a human had come through. A real, actual human! He was tall, lanky, covered in pimples and holding a book. That young man-human had gaped at Jecklyn for a few minutes before disappearing. Jecklyn didn't know what that was all about. What she did know was that the hundred-year-hole-opening of this century was happening tonight.

Jecklyn was trying to console the ache in her wings when a squarish-table-contraption attached to a chair fell into her space. She was able to look at this addition to her space for exactly .613229 seconds before she stretched her wings and-- GLORY -- flew through the hole.

As she passed between her personal Hell and Earth, an unbearable stench

hit her nostrils. Jecklyn retched and continued on her way to Heaven. She

was received wearily by the Lord and issued a stern warning to be kind.

Mrs. Sorries' senior class was filing in their classroom on a cool

November morning when Monica Kipp found herself without a desk.

Monica was a pudgy girl who lived with her creepy Uncle Al in a run-

down shack two streets down from the town dump.

"Mrs. Sorries! My desk is gone!" she cried, and the class

laughed at her. Where her desk formerly stood now sat an ugly stain,

large and brown and amoeba shaped. "My desk is gone and there's a spot

in its place!"

"Looks like you shit on the floor." The kids were mean at North

River Public School and Monica Kipp was prime pickings.

"Shut up!" Mrs. Sorries screamed. The teachers were no better

and Mrs. Sorries was six months from retirement. "Shut your mealy

mouth holes." Mrs. Sorries started the lesson and Monica Kipp had no

choice but to sit on the stain and listen.

From Heaven, Jecklyn James watched, fascinated that her black

Hell space had been under a *classroom*, of all places. She couldn't help

herself and started laughing at Monica Kipp, seated miserably atop dried

angel vomit. *What a reject!* No sooner had she thought it when a searing

pain ripped across Jecklyn's shoulders. She opened her mouth to scream as she fell, spiraling through the air, her wings ripping clear off her shoulders and leaving two large, red gashes in their wake.

She thunked down hard and this time, Jecklyn Jackson was certain the space before her was Hell.

# Wonderland

**2 a.m.**

I'm drunk again. I like the way my tongue goes numb and the way rotgut chardonnay starts to taste like Kendall Jackson or Clois du Bois after the third glass. I like the way my mind starts to wander and there are no more thoughts to be had, just ideas to spin into realities that are really dreams but I'm drunk so it does not matter.

I like to be drunk. It's a pretty good time.

I think I might like to paint or write a story but it's probably time to go to bed. I go into the re-modeled basement and only slip a little on the stairs. The stairs are carpeted with a cheap Berber over-lay my in-laws bought for my husband and I, "a Christmas gift," and I hate it. It's basically the worst gift ever. I'm glad the cats claw it every chance they get. I'm not so glad I slipped just now because I should've taken my socks off but I'm not going to. It's cold down here and I don't like cold feet.

I think maybe it's time to paint.

**4 a.m.**

There's a mural emerging on the wall. It's nice, I think. I'm surprised at how well it's coming along; you can barely tell I'm drunk from the way the lines of the rainbow explode into stars at one end. I used to paint Monday through Friday at a little sign shop downtown, but that was before the car accident and then I was drunk at work because it helped me feel better and they fired me. Insensitive pricks.

I like to be drunk because it's like another whole reality but a happy one. I'm bored now, bored with painting and with life. I think maybe there's a Percocet or a Vicodin in an old coat pocket somewhere.

When I come back up the stairs I don't slip and it feels like triumph. There are no pills, not anywhere. Maybe it's time for bed now. I could play video games, I guess.

**5 a.m.**

The kids will be up soon but this game is so entertaining. I hadn't realized how much fun playing video games could be. I wish I could play it with the kids but I can't stand being near them anymore. I am failing. They shrink when I speak, afraid I will scream at them.

I scream too much because they are loud and very annoying and I can't remember how to be patient.

**7 a.m.**

I burn the fucking scrambled eggs and smoke is everywhere and Mac comes stumbling into the kitchen drunk from sleep and I am drunk on wine and it's funny to me that we are both drunk in such different ways.

"What are you doing?" he says it very carefully, choosing his words.

"Making breakfast for the girls." I try to play it off like I've just woken up but Mac is not fooled and he's less than ecstatic.

"It's 7:00, Karen. The kids won't be up for another half an hour. Can you please just come with me?" He switches off the burner and sets the pan in the sink as I watch him. We used to have so much fun together in college; he was all I ever wanted. I have nothing to say for myself. I cannot stop laughing and Mac's face is way up near the ceiling somewhere and then I remember the pills are hidden, Mac hides the pills but I can usually find them.

I cry a little and tell him I'm sorry.

He calls his office and leaves a message that he will be late. Mac puts me to bed but he doesn't tuck me in.

"Mac?" I want to ask if he still loves me but then I remember the pills are under the mattress. Mac is highly unoriginal.

"Just…don't. Just go to sleep." He does not kiss me good night or good-bye or even good morning. I wonder if I took the time to brush my teeth if he would have kissed me.

**7:30 a.m.**

"Where's Mommy?" I haven't fallen asleep yet and I can hear the girls in the kitchen. This house is old, bought when Mac and I were just starting out, and the walls are thin. We always meant to sell it but too much happened. Kelsey is too young to realize her mother has become a drunk. Shannon is old enough to know but I think she still loves me.

"She's sick. Come and eat breakfast. Let's make the bus in time, okay?" I hear Shannon snort and imagine the look Mac gives her, half-pity and half-amusement because she's right, Mommy *is* a no good drunk. But before the guilt sets in the pills do and the guilt flies away just like Dorothy and her rainbow. Or maybe it was the witch and her bicycle.

**12:30 p.m.**

My head hurts. The house is too quiet. Why is it this quiet? Something bad must have happened, where would everyone go? I lift my head as high as I can without puking. It's past noon. I must have been up all night, drunk.

In these moments of tilted clarity, I wonder how I let myself get here. Hate myself for alienating my children and ruining my marriage. I used to be a different woman. I had the cliché of a career I loved and there were enough happy moments. But when I got into the car accident two years ago, my body was all twisted up inside my car. The pain pills weren't enough. Wine helped. And now it takes to long to feel normal.

I hate being drunk.

**1:00 p.m.**

I get out of bed, slowly. Mac has emptied my bottle. Just a sip or two of wine would have cured this pounding in my head but Mac is a sadist. There is nothing to drink anywhere and I think maybe I can find a Percocet or a Vicodin in an old jacket or a purse but my head is pounding like Santa's elves on meth.

I try my husband's cell phone and it rings three times before going to voicemail. He hit the ignore button, that bastard. I call again, and again. The ninth time I call, the cell goes straight to voicemail and I know he has turned his phone off. I call his office.

"He's in a meeting, Mrs. Abrams." That bitch secretary is lying for him; I know it. I bet it's that skinny one who looks like a glowworm with no tits. I hate her.

"It's an emergency." This woman needs to be put in her place.

"Hold, please." Her voice is cool and professional. I know she's using that voice to rub it in my face that I got fired from my job and even she, a stupid secretary, is still employed. By *my* husband. I bet they're sleeping together. Her voice is in my ear again. "I'm sorry, Mrs. Abrams, but Mr. Abrams has asked me to tell you he will call you back when he can."

I say nothing because there is nothing to say because now I know she's lying for him and this confirms it.

She's sleeping with him, that cunt.

I hang the phone up and wish it were not a cell phone so I could slam it into her ear.

**3:00 p.m.**

Mac finally called back and I told him I knew all about his affair with the secretary. He said I was delusional and he was sending me to rehab "if this doesn't stop." He hung up on me. Asshole.

Little does he know I've already been to the package store and now I can stop shaking. The girls come through the front door, home from school, and I smile at them.

"Hello." I say this very politely.

"Hi, Mommy." Kelsey hugs me and I kiss her, hold her against me for a moment. I hold my arms out to Shannon but she just looks at me and points to the bottle of wine on the counter.

That's it. "Go to your rooms. Now!" Disrespectful little brats. I twist out of Kelsey's embrace "Now!" I scream it at them. They run down the hall and two doors slam in harmony. I take another sip of wine.

My head feels pretty good even though my heart is breaking.

**7:30 p.m.**

I think I feel asleep because now it's dark outside and I can hear Mac in the kitchen, talking to the girls. I want to get up and go to them, cuddle them and say I'm sorry for screaming at them instead of smiling and making a snack but I'm too afraid to leave my bed.

When I first came home from the hospital, the girls and Mac would sit in bed with me.

It's all very sad so I cry. I cry a lot and I dry heave and give a few dramatic wails, but no one comes.

I cry by myself all the time.

**9:00 p.m.**

My first bottle of wine is gone and I'm only a few Percocet in and Mac has put the girls to bed. I've been listening very carefully all night, like a good listener should, trying to see if I can catch him on the phone with that secretary. I haven't seen him at all. He's stayed away from the bedroom all evening.

I'm sure Mac's fallen asleep on the couch and no one bothered to say good night to me.

I decide I don't care.

**12:00 a.m.**

I think maybe it's time to work on that mural. I'll add in those sparkly shoes Judy Garland wore, add them in at one end of the rainbow, underneath the stars. It will look nice, I think.

I do not slip on the stairs because I am not wearing socks but my feet are cold.

I hate to have cold feet.

**2:00 a.m.**

"Mom?" Shannon stands at the top of the basement steps and her voice makes me jump. The movement causes me to smear paint on one of the shoes. "Are you drunk again?"

"What did you just say to me?" I slam my paintbrush down. Who does she think she is? "Look at what you've done! Just look!" I walk towards her and she looks at me like *I'm* the one with the problem.

"Mom, please. Do you want to come read with me? We used to read all the time, remember?" She is sad and her voice is pleading but I am too angry. I've been working very hard on this mural.

I scream. "You go to bed! Don't talk to me like that!" I start up the steps toward her and hear footsteps coming down the hall, but Shannon just stands there like a dumb mute, crying. It's infuriating. She is ruining my alone time and I smack her, hard, because she needs to be put in her place. It is a release and it feels good so I keep going. She falls onto the floor screaming and then Mac is there.

He grabs me and slams me into the wall. Mac is shaking me and screaming in my face.

When I look over, Shannon's nose is bleeding.

Kelsey has woken up and stands in the doorway of the kitchen. I am pinned to the wall and Shannon is cowering, crawling away from me across the kitchen floor. I start to scream but I do not have words, just sounds. Mac claps his hand across my mouth and yells at the girls to go, just go to Shannon's room and lock the door behind them. And then things get confusing because I am not really sure what is happening because maybe it is a dream or maybe I am just thinking about it.

Mac pins me against the wall for a long time. I pretend he is holding me and we are about to make love. An ambulance comes and people come inside and make me go with them. I don't quite know what has happened. I think the story is over and I'm pretty sure there are no rainbows or stars or even video games.

# Another Bar Yarn

Regina Grace was more than beautiful. She was tall but it wasn't her height that was intimidating. She had calves formed from perfection and legs that made you believe in God. Her eyes spoke six different languages. She was a showstopper.

Gina was just *that girl*. Not exactly red hair, more the idea of it. She threw her head back when she laughed; a slender leg stretched provocatively toward her audience. Her left high heel dangled from a pointed toe as she stretched. Gina was aware of every eye when she snapped that heel back into place. Faint scars ran along her right jaw and heightened my intrigue of her.

The night I met her, the only time I ever saw her, we drowned ourselves in shots of Jaeger. I am now forever lost in the imaginary shadow and mystery of Regina Grace. I adored every licorice-burping minute of it.

Gina walked into the pub just after ten on a Tuesday night – an odd time for a good-looking girl in her twenties to enter a place like Harry's. We're a rough and tumble crowd, hard working guys in our fifties with nowhere to go, no families. Lonely men too manly to admit they're lonely. Harry's is a side street bar, owned by Harry himself, and it's not what you'd call well lit. It's a dirty little place tucked out of the way from the tourist part of the city. When Gina walked in, she looked around a bit before settling on the cracked leather stool beside me. She put her arms on the bar, ignored the sticky remnants born from years of spilled alcohol, and asked me to buy her a shot.

I obliged.

The men surrounding us stared like lecherous dogs. Make no mistake; I myself am one of those lecherous dogs. I just hid it better than they did that night. At first I tried to hit on her but it didn't work. I'm a man who will take what he can get.

Regina pulled out a picture after that first shot. "Look." she said.

I looked. A sullen looking guy was standing in the picture next to her, messing up what should have been a masterpiece. His face was weathered, large nose jutting out from a leathery mess of a face like a hawk's beak. Long, blonde hair. He appeared to be a simple man with a handicap: he was an amputee…the left leg. You could see it clear as day in the photo. I sat there holding the two of them on paper in my palm and snickered like a schoolboy who's seen his teacher's dress tucked up in her panties.

"What am I looking at?" I signaled Harry for another round.

"My life." She spit her words at me and snatched the picture back. "I met him last summer on Misquamicut beach."

"Aw, kid. You're pulling my leg. You must have pulled that guy's leg too hard, too." I laughed and rubbed my jaw, looking at that scar on her face. It was silver in the bar lights.

Gina didn't think that was funny. Her eyes were on fire. "I came looking for a friend. Maybe I should go."

"No, no. Stay. I'm sorry. I was just thought maybe he was your brother or something and you needed to vent."

She didn't believe me but she stayed anyway.

When she told me her story, all I could do was lust over everything I wanted her to be and steal that story for my own. That guy is dead now and I'll never see her again anyway. It doesn't matter.

Gina scooped peanuts from the bowl between us as she spoke. I wanted to warn her how many germs were loaded in that toilet bowl of peanuts, but watching her mouth work around them was too enticing. "Two summers ago, my family vacationed to Rhode Island. It's the oddest little place but beautiful. The sand is wonderful, like the kind you find in the Caribbean -- fine sand, but the waves are huge."

I nodded like I'd traveled the Caribbean my whole life.

"I would walk the beach every night. One night, a dog came running up from behind me and knocked me down. Bastard bit me right on my face." She traced the scar with her fingers and took another shot. "I just curled into a ball and prayed he wouldn't bite me again. This man finally came and got the dog to calm down. He insisted I go to the hospital. I didn't want to, but he insisted. He told me he was a nurse."

A fucking man-nurse, can you believe it?

"We wound up talking for hours in the hospital."

I interrupt her here. "What do you mean; you wound up talking for hours?"

"Just what I said." She raised an eyebrow and crushed her cigarette into the ashtray, letting the smoke unfurl from her red lips. I bought two more shots.

"Continue." I slid the shot towards her. "I want to hear the rest, Gina. I don't get how you can even speak to someone whose dog just attacked you. You ever heard of a lawyer?"

"You..." she slammed back the shot, "are an insensitive prick." She continued, telling me how she got home from the hospital and her parents were frantic. No one knew where she was and she hadn't bothered to call. She was twenty-four-years-old then, and capable of making her own decisions. Gina tried to brush the whole thing off but her mother kept touching the stitches lining Gina's jaw and shaking her head.

"But what did they say?" I asked her. "Surely your family didn't brush it aside."

"They didn't. My father told me I was an idiotic fool and my mom said my face would be disfigured. My sisters made fun of me constantly." She twisted her lips into a weird little smile. "I didn't care."

"So why were you on the family trip, anyway?"

"Free trip." she smirked at me. "I fell in love with him."

"With who?"

"James. His name was James."

"You can't fall in love in a day." I passed her another shot. "Wish you could, but it doesn't exist. And when a dog bites your face, you sue."

"No. James loved that dog. He begged me not to say anything, so I didn't. I said I cut it opening a quohaug, that the shell sliced my face when I pulled back too hard. The doctor didn't believe me but it didn't matter. We didn't go to the hospital where James worked. Seven stitches, nothing major. Toby was just playing."

"Ah, Toby." I said. "Of course, the dog must be addressed by name."

She gave me that look again, eyebrows raised. "You sound like my father. And it wasn't a day. It was instantly. I loved James instantly." I ordered another round. In my head, I was asking myself how a person could fall in love instantly. That guy was no looker. I guess to some people looks don't matter. Not to me though, nope. I'm a legs man and ugly women don't make the cut for me. No fat chicks, either. And I sure as hell would not love a girl with a dog who mauled my face.

"I walked the beach again the next night, and there he was. Toby was on a leash this time. We talked. We met every night on the beach, and eventually we went to his house." She sighed deeply, longing in her breath, and I tried not to imagine her with this amputee but the physics of how this would work had me thinking something fierce. "He was so unique. Everything sad bothered him. James took on the weight of the world. He saw too much grey and I tried to get him to see black and white. I tried to be enough for him. He would talk about world issues, poverty and hunger, and he cried for injustice." Gina had tears in her eyes but I was trying not to laugh. Not at her – at the sensitive man-nurse.

"How do you know it was love?" I had to check again.

"I just knew, okay? I loved him." Gina's voice was strangled. "Where's the bathroom in this place?" I pointed.

I didn't dare make eye contact with any of the boys while she was gone, and I know they were looking straight at me. I stared straight ahead and told them nothing until the next night.

She came back within a minute or two, not long at all for a girl, and slid back onto her barstool. I winced when she grabbed another handful of peanuts. "So anyway, he left this place after I had been home maybe a week. He called me once and we talked for three hours. He told me he would always love me." Gina looked up at me and seemed confused. "Another round?"

I obliged.

"Where'd he go?"

"Disneyland." And then she was crying and I was embarrassed but trying to show compassion, you know, this young chick at the bar crying and me sitting there all middle-aged and awkward. She stopped crying quickly enough, thank God, and Harry brought her a box of tissues and a glass of water.

"Drink this, miss, it'll help." He said it to her but was giving me a look.

"He just swam out into the ocean and never came back. Never left a note or anything." Gina was looking off to the side, somewhere else.

"An accident?"

"No." Her voice was steady.

"So how do you know?"

"They found his body."

"None of this makes sense. You take a walk, wind up with stitches in your face, fall in love with a guy you don't know, and then he kills himself? He must've just swum out too far or something. He only had one leg…maybe he got tired."

She turned to me then, and the gleam of fury in her eyes made her look like a goddess incarnate. She told me that when she met James she was transformed into something else, a better person. He told her he loved her for her mind, not her beauty. Gina told me how before, the people in her life based everything on the way she looked. James didn't. And it was as simple as that. Gina swore it was Truth.

"You know what he said to me? 'I'm a fucking amputee, all I'll do is bring you down.' I couldn't get it through his head that none of that mattered. My family hated him, hated his dog. They hated that I loved him and hated the time we spent together. He was all that could have made me happy." She heaved a huge sigh then, the biggest one yet, and asked for one last shot. "I guess I'm destined to be alone."

"You'll find someone. You're still young."

"But I couldn't save him."

"So why'd he do it, anyway? Why'd he kill himself?"

"He was depressed." She looked at me like I was an idiot. "He was always telling me he was going to do it."

"Can I ask you something?" I didn't want to ask but I had to know.

"Yes."

"How's an amputee walk on the beach?"

"You asshole."

"I guess." I said, and signaled for another round. She stood and said she was headed to the bathroom again, kissed me softly on the cheek.

"Thank you for listening. Sometimes I just need to talk and no one understands. I think you get me." I won't lie; I got a chub when she did that.

That girl was a crazy vixen, a siren of all men who were previously nothing.

"You okay?" I asked her when she got back. I wanted to lean in, caress her leg a bit but I knew she wouldn't go for it.

"I'm fine. You ready for the last round?" We clink our shot glasses together and knock back more of that harsh, licorice sweetness. "When I found out he offed himself," –those were her exact words, he offed himself – "it was something I knew would happen but I just had to wait for it."

"Damn. So why love him?" I said. I couldn't think of anything else to say.

"Couldn't help it." She ground out another cigarette, exhaled heavily, and stood up. Her scar, faint as it was, caught the light just so and gleamed silver -- her beauty in that imperfection was startling. She stood there, unsteady on her feet, and stared at me like I was something she'd never seen before.

"You okay?" I had to ask it again; I was feeling a bit over-responsible for all the shots I bought her. Harry kept glaring at me. I held that feline goddess's arm and steadied her on her feet.

"I'm fine. Just need to go. I can't…talk…about James anymore. It hurts. I need to go. Thank you for listening. You were exactly what I needed tonight."

What could I do? I walked her out to the street, pressed a twenty into her hand, and hailed a taxi.

Just like that, she was gone.

When I walked back in the bar, the scent of alcohol hit me like an assassin. I couldn't stay there. The whole night was surreal and my head was spinning. I took one look at Tom and those other dogs and changed my mind. I'd tell them everything the next day. And I did. I held court in that bar like a king, sharing a twisted story I only half-believed myself.

The night I gave her story away, I rode home alone in a cab just like always. I thought of her as I pulled up my collar and hunkered down in my seat, letting my breath fog up the glass.

Made in the USA
Middletown, DE
07 March 2021